THE LAND OF CHIMA

I am LaGravis, the king of the Lions. We are one of many animal tribes that live in the magical kingdom of Chima. It is the Lions' duty to maintain peace and balance throughout the land.

We weren't always the advanced and sophisticated creatures we are now. Centuries ago, all the animals in Chima were simple and pure. Then, one day, the sky opened up and a bolt of lightning struck the ground. Earthquakes shook. Tornadoes whirled across the sky. And a magical rock called Mount Cavora rose into the air.

The water that spilled from this floating mountain was full of a life-force we now call CHI. The Lions drank from it first. Then the other animals followed. We became smarter, move evolved. And as we changed, our world changed, too. . . .

ANIMAL KINGDOM

Mount Cavora still supplies us with CHI today. Thanks to its incredible energy, our ancestors built amazing vehicles and developed advanced technology. We—the inhabitants of Chima—rely on CHI, because it powers everything we have created. CHI Orbs greatly enhance an animal's strength, abilities, and instincts. But its power only lasts for a few hours.

THE CHI

CHI is collected at the Lion Temple. It forms into powerful orbs, thanks to special minerals in the Sacred Pool. As the first creatures to drink CHI, we Lions are its guardians, ensuring that it is shared fairly by all. Once a month, we distribute the orbs to every tribe in Chima—even those tribes we may not agree with.

THE TOURNAMENT

Each month, there's always one extra-powerful Golden Orb of CHI. Unlike normal CHI, it keeps its incredible energy forever. But it is not simply given away. The citizens of Chima compete for it in a monthly tournament at the Grand Arena. Golden CHI has the power to transform the arena and choose a different contest each month—jousting, racing, or acrobatics—so that no one tribe has an advantage in winning it. Victory is a source of tribal pride for weeks following the contest.

THE TRIBES

There are many other tribes in Chima, including the Crocodiles, the Eagles, the Wolves, the Gorillas, the Ravens, the Rhinos, and the Bears. For a thousand years, all the tribes worked together side by side and lived in peace and harmony. That is, until the battle began for control of the CHI . . .

ALLIES AND ENEMIES

When the Crocodiles lost their king, Crominus, in an accident, the king's son, Cragger, took his place. The young and ambitious prince followed the advice of his scheming sister, Crooler, and decided that his tribe should control the CHI. The Wolves and the Ravens joined them, and together they challenged the Lions. The Eagles and the Gorillas stood by the Lions to protect Chima's greatest treasure from falling into the greedy claws of the enemy.

THE LIONS

We Lions strongly believe in tradition and rules. For us, it is important to always be fair and just. Even if we are at odds with another tribe, we will still give them their equal share of CHI each month. We do this not only for ourselves, but for the sake of all of Chima.

LAVAL

One day my son, Laval, will become a great warrior and leader. But for now, he still has a lot to learn. He understands that our rules are important. But he sometimes puts "having fun" ahead of following them. Laval is very headstrong, curious, and loves adventure. I can see how he struggles daily with obeying all of our rules. But I have faith that my son will soon learn to sacrifice his own wants for the greater good.

LENNOX

Lennox is a brave young foot soldier with the heart of a great warrior. He drives the powerful Lion Attack vehicle and loves it more than anything. In his spare time, Lennox makes special modifications to his vehicle and practices combat maneuvers in the jungle. Everyone wonders how the nature-loving Gorillas don't seem to mind Lennox's wild and roaring joyrides.

LONGTOOTH

Longtooth is one of my oldest and most trusted soldiers. He once refused to join the tribal elders because he said he loved the "action" of the frontlines too much. The truth is Longtooth loves *talking* about action more than pursuing it. He has far too many aches and pains to be in battle often. Still, he can always be counted on to defend the Lion Temple . . . as long as his back doesn't give out.

LEONIDAS

Leonidas is another of my most valued guards. He is vigilant and fierce, though at times he can get confused. If you ordered him to guard the Temple entrance, he would do so without question. But if you asked him to clean his sword at the same time, he couldn't hold the two ideas in his head at once. He is a Lion who actually *can't* chew gum and walk at the same time.

SPEEDOR RACERS

The Speedor is the most popular vehicle in Chima. Its wheel is carved from rare Tribe Stones that fell off Mount Cavora centuries ago. Since the wheel is a part of nature, it draws its energy from growing plants. This is why it can zip through lush jungles but struggles to move in barren deserts.

Only one of the pictures below matches the image of Leonidas riding his Speedor. Which one?

A   B   C   D   E

The Wolves have joined the Crocodiles in the battle to take control of all the CHI! Can you spot five differences between the two images below?

KNEE-DEEP TROUBLE

ROARING LION VEHICLES

It's not easy to travel across rugged land even if you are an animal. So the Lion Engineers constructed powerful vehicles. Built in times of peace, they have become very useful in battles against the Crocodiles.

QUICK QUIZ

Which tribe is responsible for fair distribution of CHI Orbs?

LENNOX'S LION ATTACK

The trademark of any Lion Vehicle is the design of a Lion's head on the front. Lennox's Lion Attack is a proud-looking all-terrain vehicle that is both light and sturdy. It is mainly used for scouting missions, but it can be used for transportation when necessary. Watch out when Lennox is at the wheel. With its CHI-powered claws, nothing can stop it!

LAVAL'S ROYAL HUNTER

Thanks to its CHI powered engines and four big tracks, this sturdy vehicle can rumble through any terrain. It was designed for hunting expeditions, but with a few modifications it has turned into a powerful battle machine. The front frame is shaped like a Lion's head and not only scares away enemies but also opens to reveal a hidden compartment. This vehicle has room for a driver in the cockpit and a controller in the CHI canon tower, usually operated by the Lion Prince himself.

MEMORY QUIZ

The technology of the Lion Tribe is truly impressive! What do you remember about the two vehicles described on pages 10–11? Read the sentences and mark them "T" for "TRUE" or "F" for "FALSE".

LENNOX'S LION ATTACK

1. *It is Laval's favorite vehicle.*
2. *It is used for scouting missions.*
3. *Its front is shaped like a lion's paw.*
4. *It is armed with CHI-powered claws.*
5. *It can travel on any terrain.*

LAVAL'S ROYAL HUNTER

1. *It is big, heavy, and very slow.*
2. *It has two sun-powered engines.*
3. *It rides on four big tracks.*
4. *It was designed for hunting.*
5. *It has an elevated canon tower.*

DRAW THE LION PRINCE

In the battle against the Crocodiles, Laval is a fierce warrior. Cop details of the portrait of Laval practicing his combat moves below ont grid to finish the picture.

The morning stillness was broken by the sound of running feet crashing through the bushes.

"You won't get away this time!" Laval shouted as he and his Lion Troops chased a group of Crocodiles deep into the jungle.

Cragger, the Crocodile King, snarled back. "Just watch us!"

The sneaky Crocodile chuckled to himself. His plan was working perfectly. Earlier that morning, Cragger and his troops had attacked the monthly CHI market. They had pretended they wanted to steal extra CHI from the Eagles and Gorillas.

But secretly, Cragger had another plan in mind. He knew that Laval would insist on chasing them. And that was just what Cragger wanted.

"What's the matter, Laval?" Cragger taunted. "Paws too soft for running fast through the jungle?"

"Just you wait," Laval said. "When we catch you, you're—*whoa!*"

Laval and his troops skidded to a halt. The ground had suddenly turned muddy. The Crocodiles had led them to the Croc Swamp!

"Something wrong?" Cragger laughed as he dove into the murky water.

Laval turned to the other Lions. Something *was* wrong. Laval didn't know how to swim. If he went into the swamp, he could drown.

"What should we do, Prince Laval?" one of his soldiers asked.

Before Laval could answer, Cragger cried out, "Release the gate!"

Instantly, four Crocs slashed thick vines holding back a large gate made out of swamp branches. A flood of water rushed out, surrounding the muddy patch Laval and the Lions were standing on. They were trapped!

"Let's see you get away now, Laval," Cragger sneered.

The Lions looked at one another. This was not good. Even the best of them wasn't a strong swimmer. If they went into the swamp, the Crocs would attack for sure.

"Maybe we could make a bridge out of swamp grass?" one of the Lion Warriors suggested.

Laval shook his head. "No, it won't be strong enough to hold us. We need another plan."

But as the stinky swamp water inched closer, Laval grew worried.

There was no way for the Lions to defend themselves if the Crocs attacked them in the swamp. They would be helpless.

"That's right, take your time," the Crocodiles teased from the center of the swamp. They splashed around and dove in and out of the water. "By the time you come up with a plan, it will be too late!"

"Any ideas?" Laval asked the Lions. But they all shook their heads.

"There must be a way to get out of this," Laval muttered. He couldn't help being angry with himself. His father, King LaGravis, would have told him to keep a cool head when the Crocs attacked. Laval shouldn't have chased after them with such a small group of Lions. They were in danger now, and it was Laval's fault.

His father and the other tribes didn't even know where they were. . . .

"They don't know where we are," Laval said slowly. "That's it!"

He turned to his troops. "I think I know a way out," Laval said. "The other tribes are sure to be looking for us. We need to get to the top of these trees and signal for help."

"But the swamp water is closing in fast," one of his soldiers pointed out.

"Then we only have one shot," Laval said, determined. "Get on my shoulders and jump to the nearest tree. When you reach the top, see if you can spot any of the Eagles. It's our only chance."

Quickly, the Lion Soldier hopped onto Laval's shoulders and made a flying leap. He just reached the nearest tree! The swamp water gurgled at his feet as he started to climb.

Cragger saw what was happening and snarled. "Enough messing around," he exclaimed. "Let's finish this."

The Crocs began swimming toward the trapped Lions.

"Now would be the time for some good news!" Laval called up as he and his other soldiers prepared to fight.

"I see them!" the Lion called down. "The Eagles—they're looking for us." He waved his arms. "Over here—hurry!"

The Eagles spotted them right away. "Laval!" cried Eris the Eagle. "We're coming! Hang on!"

In a flash, the Eagles swooped down to lift the Lions one by one from the jungle. It was just in time, too. The Crocs had just reached them!

"Sorry we can't stick around, guys," Laval said as the Eagles grabbed the last of them. "Maybe next time!"

Cragger growled. "You got lucky this time, Laval. Next time, you won't be!"

Laval smiled gratefully up at Eris as they flew home. "Thanks, Eris," he said. "I owe you one."

Eris laughed. "Next time, just don't let your temper get the best of you," she said. "It landed you in deep trouble."

"You can say that again." Laval nodded. "Swamp-deep trouble!"

TRUE OR FALSE

The adventure might have turned out badly for Laval and his loyal warriors without the help of their Eagle friends. Read the sentences about the story and mark the true ones with "T" and the false ones with "F."

1. *The Lions played hide-and-seek with the Crocodiles.*

2. *The Crocodiles stole a lot of CHI Orbs from the Lion Temple.*

3. *Cragger's plan was really to trap the Lions in the swamp.*

4. *Laval is a great swimmer.*

5. *The Lions built a bridge out of swamp grass.*

6. *Eris and other Eagles lifted the Lions to safety.*

ERIS'S SECRET

Unlike many other Eagles, Eris is always focused and quick-witted. This is why she spends a lot of time with her earth-bound friends, like Laval. She is also a great fighter. What she lacks in strength she makes up for with brilliant tactics. But Eris dislikes conflict, and she wants peace to be restored in Chima.

Use the key to read the encoded message and discover Eris's secret.

A C E
H I L
N O R
S U V

THE EAGLES

The members of the Eagle tribe live in quirky cliff dwellings that cling to the sides of Chima's mysterious rock spires. They are wise thinkers and can launch fierce aerial assaults when needed. Just don't get them started talking, or you may have to listen to their offbeat philosophical theories for hours.

EWALD

Ewald is the leader of the wise elders who form the Eagle Tribe's Ruling Council. He is prone to endless debates about everything from battle strategy to what the Eagles should eat for lunch. He is always searching for the perfect solutions to problems, which keeps him from accomplishing anything. The truth is, he loves the debate about action far more than the action itself.

EWAR

Ewar's responsibility is to uphold peace and order in the Eagle Territory. He is in charge of the Eagles' castle guards. He claims that under his warriors' watchful eyes even a mouse would not slip into the castle (unless, of course, the guards are busy discussing issues such as, "Is the glass of water half empty or half full?").

EQUILA

Like any other Eagle, Equila is a bit scatter-brained. However, this particular bird is both a fast flyer and a fast talker. These traits make him a natural announcer when the races for the Golden CHI are on. In difficult times, though, Equila proves to be one of the strongest Eagle Warriors. He fights bravely in the air and on land—especially when piloting the Eagles' awesome ground-driven vehicles.

EGLOR

Eglor is a master of technology and rocketry. He is the Eagles' "gadget-bird" and invents many amazing new weapons. However, there is one slight problem with Eglor's work: His inventions often take too long to finish. Once, during a battle, the weapon he was inventing took so long to complete that by the time it was ready, the battle was over and all the warriors had gone home!

CHI POWER

Although they can fly, the Eagles have built machines that fly, too. Equila's modified Speedor is one great example. Equipped with two CHI-powered propellers, the vehicle speeds through the sky, saving its winged rider a lot of effort. Which of the three images at the bottom of the page is a mirror reflection of the big picture?

A   B   C

WORDSEARCH

There are 10 names of the Lions and the Eagles hidden in this grid. How fast can you find them? How many times does CHIMA appear in this wordsearch? Be careful: The words can be written across, up or down, diagonally, and backward.

```
A B G C H I M A S W E R T B N M S D A W D C D P
H L J S D A W E C V B A G C H I M A U I P H W T
L A G R A V I S K S E E D F T C A B N A M I H C
H V B G D C A J V Y R M F R O K L E T O D M P E
T A N E R H P L R I V B C S O W E Y K F U A K G
B L E O N I D A S N R T H U T K P K X B C X L L
A T L E G M T A A O P H I G G H E E R O T Y R O
M G K O E A N E W A R L M N N R J W T J N K T R
I B H M R T Y E F B V L A M O T U O A Y M N H N
H H A L I U Q E Y M W E H D L G K P K L E S E D
C N D H A J K I C H I M A F P W A S D E D E R L
```

QUICK QUIZ

Whose side are the Eagles on?

CHIMA

MECHANICAL BIRD

Eris's Royal Interceptor is a flying battle machine designed by the Eagle Tribe for guarding the skies of Chima. Thanks to its incredible speed, it can chase down any flying machine used by the Ravens. The Interceptor is equipped with many CHI-powered missiles, but its fearsome look is often enough to make the enemy think twice during an aerial combat.

QUICK QUIZ

How many claws does the Interceptor have at each leg?

PIECE TO PIECE

The great picture of Eris's Royal Interceptor from the previous page has been cut into pieces and scattered. Can you put the pieces back together? All you have to do is to write their numbers into the grid in the correct order.

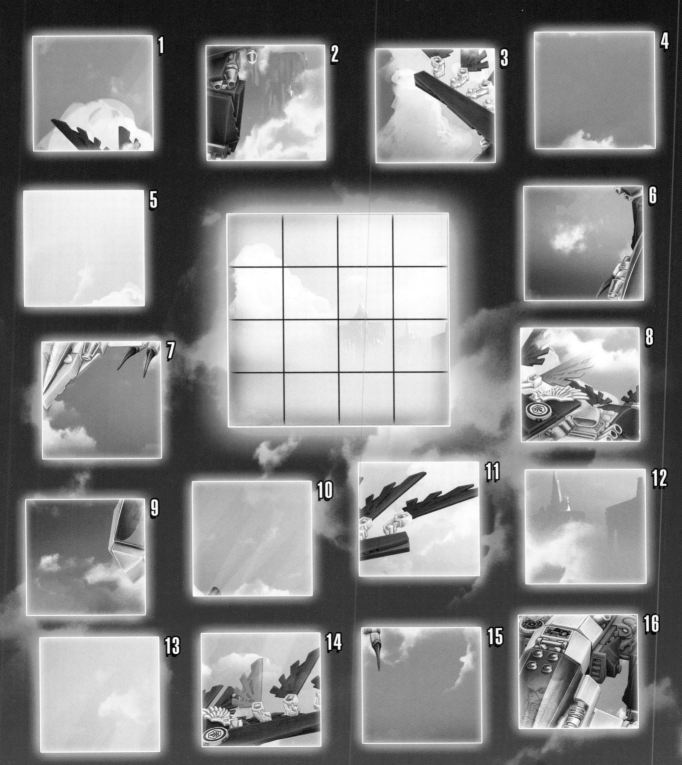

EGLOR'S MISSION

The sneaky Ravens have stolen some CHI Orbs! Help Eglor fly to their nest to retrieve the precious CHI. Guide the bold Eagle Warrior through the maze, but watch out for Ravens. There are too many of them to risk a battle!

ERIS! LENNOX! GUESS WHAT? I BUMPED INTO A WHOLE PACK OF WOLVES THE OTHER DAY. I GAVE A MIGHTY ROAR, I SWUNG MY SWORD, AND I CHASED THEM AWAY. ALL TWENTY OF THEM!

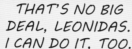

THAT'S NO BIG DEAL, LEONIDAS. I CAN DO IT, TOO.

YOU CAN FIGHT LIKE ME?

NO . . .

. . . BRAG LIKE YOU!

CHIMA QUIZ

There is a lot more to discover about the amazing Kingdom of Chima. But now it is time to test your memory of what you have learned so far. Read the quiz questions and choose one answer to each of them.

1. What were the inhabitants of Chima like centuries ago?
  A) They were simple, wild animals.
  B) They were creatures made of light.
  C) They were constantly thirsty.

2. How does CHI get into the Sacred Pool?
  A) It flows in the water that spills from Mount Cavora.
  B) It falls into it with the rocks from Mount Cavora.
  C) It is brought to it by a monthly tornado.

3. Who guards and distributes CHI fairly to all the tribes?
  A) The Eagles
  B) The Ravens
  C) The Lions

4. What effect does CHI have on an inhabitant of Chima?
  A) It enhances their strength, abilities, and instincts.
  B) It makes them walk on all fours.
  C) It makes them completely confused.

5. How often is the Golden CHI tournament organized?
  A) Once a year
  B) Once a month
  C) Once in a blue moon

6. How does the powerful Golden CHI affect the competition?
  A) It favors some competitors and helps them win.
  B) It transforms the arena to choose the type of contest.
  C) It prevents the competitors from using unlawful tricks.

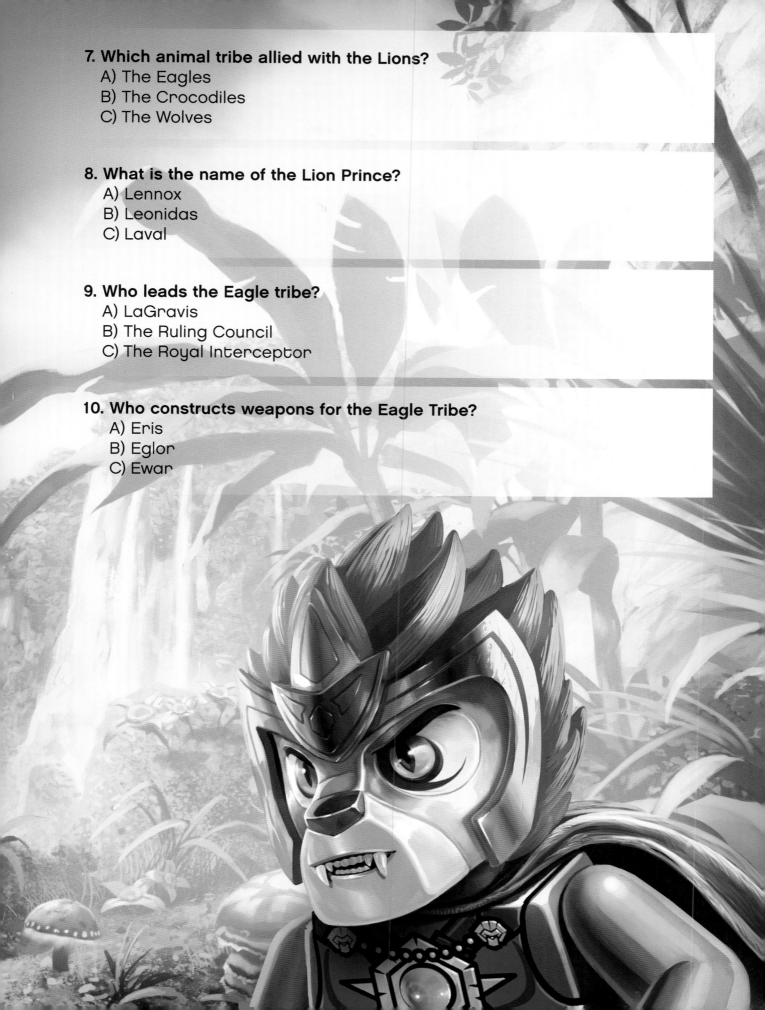

7. Which animal tribe allied with the Lions?
   A) The Eagles
   B) The Crocodiles
   C) The Wolves

8. What is the name of the Lion Prince?
   A) Lennox
   B) Leonidas
   C) Laval

9. Who leads the Eagle tribe?
   A) LaGravis
   B) The Ruling Council
   C) The Royal Interceptor

10. Who constructs weapons for the Eagle Tribe?
   A) Eris
   B) Eglor
   C) Ewar

ANSWERS

Quick Quiz

Pg. 6 Speedor Racers
Picture **D**

Pg. 7 Spot the Difference

Pg. 12 Memory Quiz

Lennox's Lion Attack
1. F, 2. T, 3. F, 4. T, 5. T

Laval's Royal Hunter
1. F, 2. F, 3. T, 4. T, 5. T

Pg. 18 True or False

1. F, 2. F, 3. T, 4. F, 5. F, 6. T

Pg. 19 Eris's Secret

Eris has a crush on Laval.

Pg. 22 CHI Power
Picture **C**

Pg. 23 Wordsearch

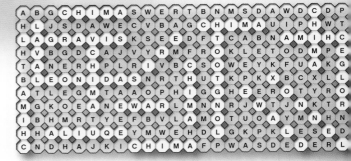

CHIMA: **8**

Pg. 25 Piece to Piece

Pg. 26 Eglor's Mission

Pg. 28-29 Chima Quiz
1. A, 2. A, 3. C, 4. A, 5. B,
6. B, 7. A, 8. C, 9. B, 10. B